To Olivia & Ella!

x o x o

♡

Francis

Francis
Goes to School

To Roy Thorp ("The Professor")
whose life was an example
of the power of love.

Francis Goes to School

Story Copyright © 2015 by Tim Dawdy
Illustrations Copyright © 2015 by Katherine Nitsch

The art was done with sketching and colored pencils. The text was set in Optima.

Printed in the United States of America

Summary: *Francis Goes to School* is the story of a bear caught up in the school system. Francis the Bear does his best in a world designed for humans. Francis is able to triumph because he's a bear!

ISBN: 978-0-9831552-7-0
Library of Congress Control Number: 2014950660

Published by The Silloway Press, Beaverton, OR
www.SillowayPress.com
Francis@SillowayPress.com

Francis
Goes to School

Story by Tim Dawdy
Illustrations by Katherine Nitsch

The Silloway Press
Beaverton, OR

Francis is a very happy bear!

Francis lives in a house with nice human parents.

He lives with his family in Fir Creek, Oregon.

Sammy the Cat also lives with Francis

and his family.

Sammy likes catching mice.

Francis helps out by vacuuming.

Their home is cheery with lots of musical instruments

and song books.

Francis enjoys gardening with his family.

Berry plants are his favorite.

Francis has lots of good food to eat.

His parents make sure that he eats a wide

variety of foods.

Eating is very important to Francis

because he's a bear.

One day, Francis's parents get a letter from the Fir
Creek School Board.

The letter says that Francis is subject to compulsory
school attendance.

"That's impossible," his parents say,

"because he's a bear!"

The parents schedule a meeting with the school board to explain that Francis is a bear, but the meeting does not go well.

The School Board will not listen. They say he is just a special little boy.

Francis's parents tell the School Board, "He's a bear!"

So now Francis is enrolled in Fir Creek
Elementary School.

He likes the kids and teachers and he doesn't mind
that he's the only bear in school.

Indeed, no one seems to notice that he's a bear.

Francis has a locker at school. All the lockers look the same.

Francis uses his powerful sense of smell to help him find his locker.

His nose is very keen because he's a bear.

Francis has a busy school schedule.

He has home room, physical education,

computer lab, and band.

But Francis likes geography class best.

He has a good sense of direction because

he's a bear.

Francis tries to say the Pledge of Allegiance, but it comes out Growl, Snarl, Snarl, Growl, and Growl. He can't talk because he's a bear.

Francis goes to speech therapy to work on his sounds but it is difficult for him, so they practice gestures, signing, and typing. Of course he snorts and growls really well because he's a bear.

Francis really likes lunch. A school lunch costs $2.00. Francis spends $20.00 a day for lunch because he eats ten school lunches every day! Francis eats so much that the cafeteria cooks think that the school has added another class.

He eats a lot because he's a bear.

Francis can't hold a pencil or a pen because he
doesn't have thumbs.

But Francis can use a computer keyboard, he just
extends his claws a little and types away.

Francis volunteers at the school library twice a week.

He enjoys helping students find books.

The library is a quiet and peaceful place.

No one asks Francis to talk in the library.

Francis plays the tuba in the school band. The tuba
takes great strength and lots of air.
Francis has both qualities because he's a bear.

Francis likes physical education class. He can run fast for a short distance, he is a good climber, and a champion wrestler.

Francis only uses one wrestling hold: the Bear Hug! He just holds his opponents in his powerful arms until they give up. Francis is always careful to keep his claws in so he never hurts anyone.

Francis's friends on the school wrestling team ask
him to run for student council.
But Francis declines the nomination because he
would have to make speeches.
Francis can't make speeches because he's a bear.

Francis does his homework after school.

Sammy chases mice while Francis studies.

Francis is a good reader, which is amazing because

he's a bear.

Dinner time is an important time at Francis's house. Everyone in the family shares what happened in their day. Francis uses his signing and gestures to share. Francis likes the food because he's a bear.

Before bed, Francis and Sammy enjoy studying
maps. They dream of far away places.
Francis wonders what kind of food they eat
in Morocco.

After a busy day, Francis has a night of peaceful rest.

Sammy likes sleeping with Francis on the fluffy bed.

Francis was afraid to go to school at first. But now, Francis enjoys the school day. Francis has learned that he can do many things well. Very often the hardest things to do are also the best things to do. Especially if you're a bear!

Meet the Author and Illustrator

Tim Dawdy works as a Battalion Chief and Public Information Officer in a suburban fire district in Washingon State.

He is an accomplished musician and singer who plays in bands in the Pacific Northwest. Tim's poetry and stories are often performed in his home town of Ridgefield, Washington.

Tim has been telling Francis stories for more than 30 years.

Katherine Nitsch works and plays in the Pacific Northwest, and is a retired speech language pathologist from the Battle Ground school district. With her speech therapy groups, the classroom white board was her favorite palette to help illustrate ideas.

She is a singer and guitar player in a band (Misty Mamas). Katherine enjoys kayaking, writing, biking, and gardening in her Vancouver, WA home.

CPSIA information can be obtained at www.ICGtesting.com
Printed in the USA
LVOW02*1929011114

411202LV00002B/2/P